MINI CLASSICS

THE
EMPEROR'S
NEW CLOTHES

© Parragon Book Service Ltd

This edition printed for:
Shooting Star Press, Inc.
230 Fifth Avenue–Suite 1212,
New York, NY 10001

Shooting Star Press books are available at special
discounts for bulk purchases for sales promotions,
premiums, fund-raising, or educational use. Special
editions or book excerpts can also be created to
specification. For details contact: Special Sales
Director, Shooting Star Press, Inc., 230 Fifth Avenue,
Suite 1212, New York, New York 10001.

ISBN 1 56924 208 9

Printed and bound in Great Britain.

MINI CLASSICS

THE
EMPEROR'S
NEW CLOTHES

RETOLD BY STEPHANIE LASLETT
ILLUSTRATED BY RODNEY SHAW

SHOOTING STAR PRESS

Many years ago, in a country far away, there lived an Emperor who was so fond of new clothes that he spent all his money on them in order to be beautifully dressed at all times.

He was not interested in his soldiers. He didn't care for the theatre. No, *this* Emperor liked nothing better than to walk about in his new clothes, showing off to anyone who might care to watch.

He had a different outfit for every hour of the day, and happily changed his clothes each morning, afternoon and evening. He was never to be found in his Council Chamber talking to his ministers.

"The Emperor is busy in his dressing room," they would be told.

The great city in which he lived was large and prosperous. Every day many strangers came to visit the bustling town.

One day two men
arrived at the city gate.

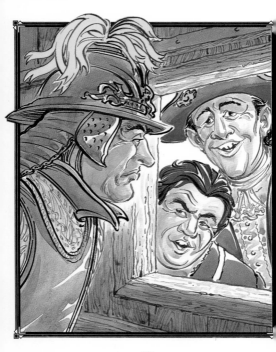

They were dishonest
swindlers pretending to
be weavers.

"We can weave a cloth
more beautiful than you
could ever imagine," they
said. "Such wonderful
patterns! Such rich texture!"

Then the swindlers explained that, as well as being the most exquisite material ever seen, this cloth had special magic properties.

"It will seem invisible to stupid and foolish people," they claimed. "Only those who are clever will be able to see it." When the Emperor heard the news, he was very impressed. "These must indeed be splendid clothes," he thought. "When I wear them I can find out which of my ministers are incapable of carrying out important duties. I can find out who is wise and who is stupid!

"I would dearly love a suit like that. This cloth must be woven for me at once." And the Emperor gave both the imposters a large bag full of money so that they could begin their work at once.

They set up their two weaving looms and began to work. Back and forth went their shuttles as the two men bent over the looms — but there was no thread and no cloth to be seen!

Their weaving looms were completely bare. The weavers went to the Emperor and asked for the finest silk and the best gold thread, then they secretly hid these riches in their pockets.

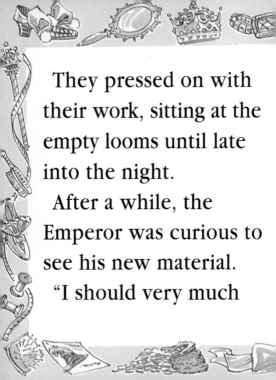

They pressed on with their work, sitting at the empty looms until late into the night.

After a while, the Emperor was curious to see his new material.

"I should very much

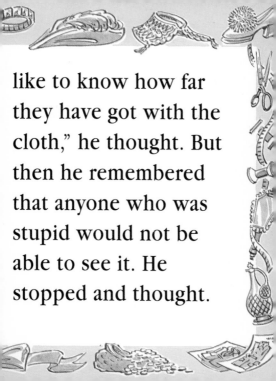

like to know how far
they have got with the
cloth," he thought. But
then he remembered
that anyone who was
stupid would not be
able to see it. He
stopped and thought.

"Well, I know *I* will be clever enough to see the cloth," said the Emperor to himself, "but this will give me a wonderful opportunity to see how intelligent my Prime Minister is. He will be able to judge the cloth and tell me what he thinks of it."

And so the old Prime Minister went into the hall where the two imposters sat working at the empty weaving looms.

"Dear me!" thought the old man, opening his eyes wide—for he could see no cloth at all!

The swindlers begged him to be so kind as to step closer, and inspect their hard work.

"Feel this wonderful texture," they exclaimed. "Look at these lovely colours." They pointed to the empty looms and the poor old Prime Minister went forward rubbing his eyes. But

still he could see nothing,
for the very good reason
that there was nothing
there to see!

"Dear, dear!" he thought
to himself. "Am I stupid?
I didn't think I was!
Nobody must find out.

"No, I certainly must not admit that I cannot see the cloth!"

"Have you nothing to say about our cloth?" asked one of the men.

"Oh, it is lovely, most lovely!" answered the Prime Minister, hurriedly. He looked closely through his spectacles. "Such exture! What colours!" he exclaimed. "Yes, I will ell the Emperor that it pleases me very much."

"We are delighted to hear it," said both the weavers as they winked at one another.

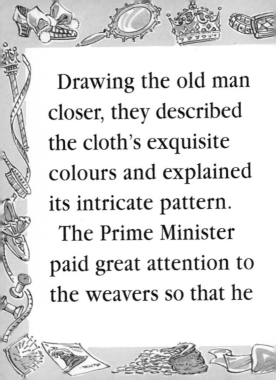

Drawing the old man closer, they described the cloth's exquisite colours and explained its intricate pattern.

The Prime Minister paid great attention to the weavers so that he could repeat everything he heard to the Emperor when he returned. After the old man had left the room, the two swindlers laughed and laughed.

"We certainly fooled him!" they said.

Soon the imposters said
they wanted more money
and more silk and gold
to use in their weaving.
But, as before, they put
the silk and gold thread
in their own pockets,
and there was still no
sign of any cloth at all!

And day after day the weavers carried on pretending to work.

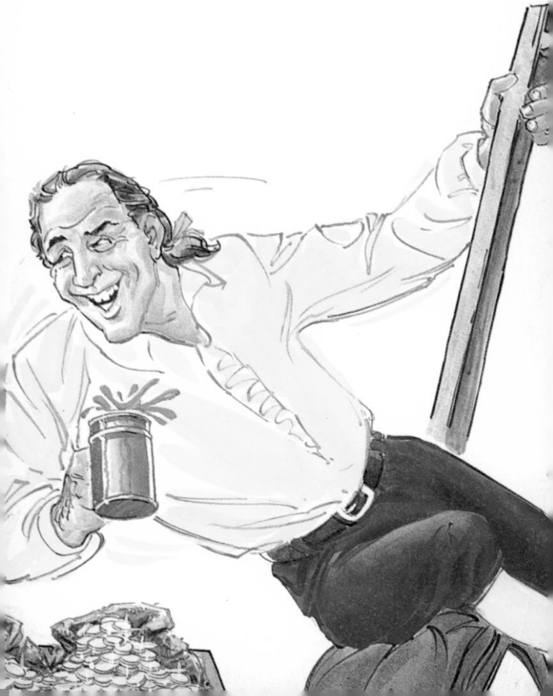

Time passed and the Emperor decided to send another of his ministers to see how the weaving was progressing, and whether the cloth would soon be finished. "I will send my Chancellor," he thought. "He is a wise and clever man. He will give me a reliable report."

But when the Chancellor arrived to inspect the cloth he, too, could see nothing at all. Nervously, he stood and bit his lip.

"Is it not a beautiful piece of cloth?" asked the two imposters, as they pointed to the splendid length of material which was not there.

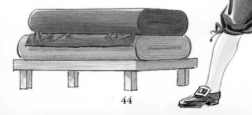

"I am not stupid!" thought the Chancellor, "but if I cannot see the cloth then it must mean that I am unfit for my position. How terrible! No-one must know that I cannot see the cloth!"

And so he praised the cloth which he could not see, and expressed great delight at the beautiful colours and the splendid texture.

"Yes, it is quite lovely," he told the Emperor, and

back in their room, the
two weavers hugged
themselves with glee.
  Soon everybody in
town was talking about
the magnificent cloth
being woven for the
Emperor's new clothes.

Itching with impatience,
the excited Emperor
could wait no longer.

He wanted to see the cloth for himself while it was still on the loom.

Off he marched, with a great crowd of curious courtiers and ministers jostling behind him, including the Chancellor and Prime Minister who had already given him such glowing reports.

The Emperor entered the room to find the cunning imposters busily weaving with all their might, but without an inch of thread on their empty looms.

"Is it not splendid!" said

the two old statesmen.
"See, your Majesty! Such
texture! What colours!"
And then they pointed
to the loom, for they
believed that the others
would be able to see the
cloth perfectly well.

"What!" thought the Emperor in dismay. "I can see nothing! This is terrible! Am I stupid? Am I not fit to be Emperor? That would be quite unthinkable! I *must* be Emperor. I *must*!"

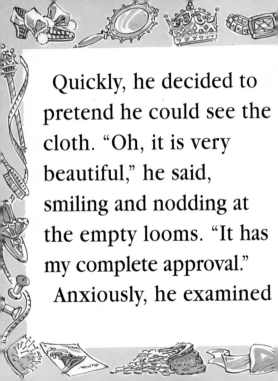

Quickly, he decided to pretend he could see the cloth. "Oh, it is very beautiful," he said, smiling and nodding at the empty looms. "It has my complete approval."

Anxiously, he examined

the empty looms, for he
could not believe that he
saw nothing at all.

Puzzled, his whole
Court gathered round
and stared. They, too,
saw nothing but did not
want to appear stupid.

With one voice they echoed the Emperor's words. "Oh! It is beautiful! Exquisite! Superb!"

And they advised him to wear this new and magnificent cloth at the grand procession which was to take place the very next day.

"Splendid! Lovely! Most beautiful!" said all the

Emperor's courtiers who seemed quite delighted with the weavers.

The Emperor heartily congratulated them and awarded them the title "Court Weavers to the Emperor."

All through the night,
the weavers sat and
worked on the Emperor's
new clothes. They burned
over sixteen candles on
their windowsill so that
anyone watching could
see how busy they were.

First the weavers
pretended to take the
cloth from the loom.
Then with huge scissors
they cut out their pattern.

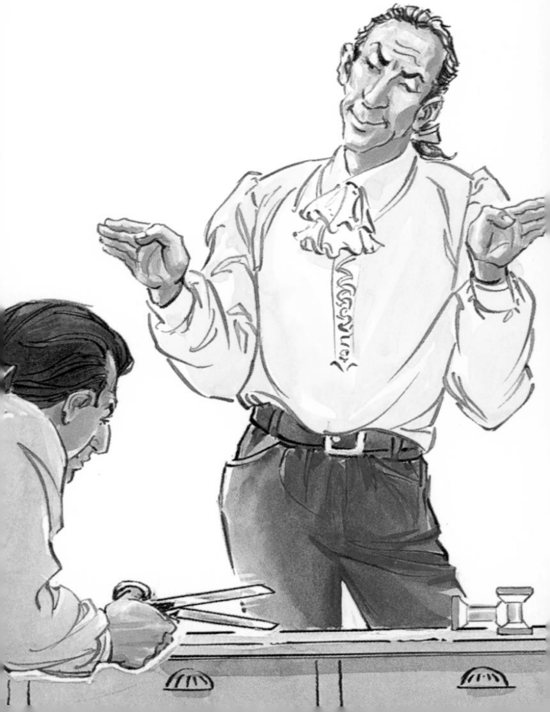

Next they threaded
their needles (with no
thread!) and sewed the
pieces together. Then at
last they announced,
"The suit is finished!"

Along came the vain
Emperor with all his
courtiers and ministers.
As they crowded into
the room, the weavers
held out their arms as if
holding up something
very delicate and precious.

"See! Here are your breeches, Your Majesty," they said. "Here is your coat! And here is your fine cloak! This special cloth is so comfortable that you will feel as if you are wearing nothing at all — but that is the beauty of it!" Everyone murmured in approval. "Yes, of course," said all his ministers, but really they could see nothing, for there was nothing there to see.

"Will it please Your Majesty to take off your clothes," said the imposters, "then we will dress you in your suit, here before the mirror."

So the Emperor took off all his clothes and the imposters pretended to dress him in his fine new outfit.

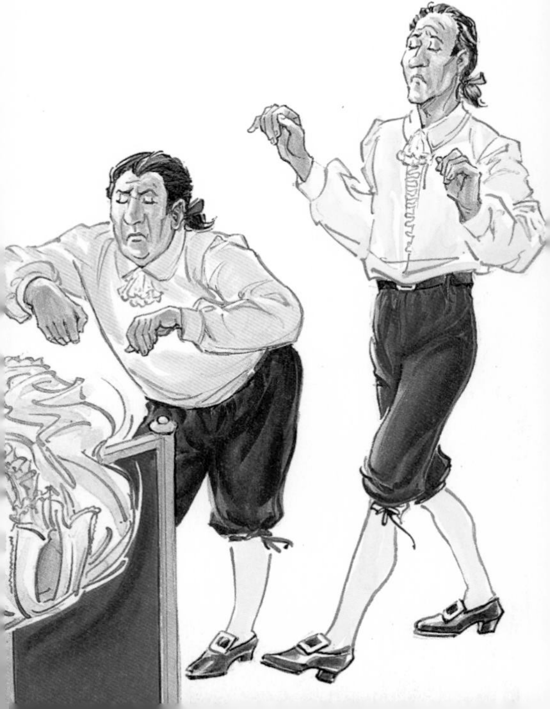

The Emperor twisted
and turned the better to
admire himself in front
of the mirror.

"What a perfect fit!"
everyone exclaimed.
"Such colours! It is
indeed a gorgeous suit!"

"Everything is ready for the procession, Your Majesty," announced the Master of Ceremonies.

"I have finished dressing,"
said the Emperor, as he
strutted before them.
"Don't I look grand!"

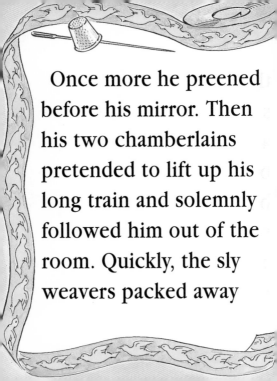

Once more he preened before his mirror. Then his two chamberlains pretended to lift up his long train and solemnly followed him out of the room. Quickly, the sly weavers packed away their looms and their shuttles, their scissors and their needles, their bags of money and their bundles of silk and gold thread and they ran away, never to be seen in that fair city again!

Outside in the bright
sunshine the Emperor
walked in a dignified
and stately fashion at the

head of the grand
procession, and all the
people stared as he
slowly marched by.

Stifling their horrified gasps, they could see he was wearing not a stitch of clothing! But no-one dared admit such a thing, for each of them feared they would then be considered foolish.

"Look at the Emperor's new clothes!" they cried. "Look at the magnificent train! Such exquisitely beautiful cloth!"

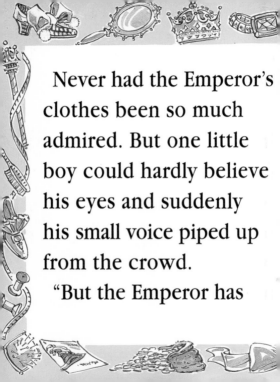

Never had the Emperor's clothes been so much admired. But one little boy could hardly believe his eyes and suddenly his small voice piped up from the crowd.

"But the Emperor has

nothing on!" he laughed.
"Just listen to the
innocent child!" said his
father. "Hush, hush, my
boy!" But soon everyone
nearby was repeating
what the honest child
had said.

"He has nothing on!" they whispered to each other until at last the whole crowd cried out, "But he has nothing on!" Then the Emperor trembled and knew they were speaking the truth.

There he was at the head of the procession wearing no clothes at all! But he was too proud to admit his foolish vanity and, with his nose in the air and a straight back, he marched on under his splendid canopy. And marching behind him, with even straighter backs, were his poor chamberlains, still tightly holding on to the invisible train...

HANS CHRISTIAN ANDERSEN

Hans Christian Andersen was born in
Odense, Denmark, on April 2nd, 1805.
His family was very poor and throughout his
life he suffered much unhappiness. Even after
he had found success as a writer, Andersen felt
something of an outsider, an aspect which
often emerged in his stories. *The Emperor's
New Clothes* is an unforgettable story enjoyed
by every child, but Andersen would also
have enjoyed the chance it gave him to make
fun of the rigid class system and the
hypocrisy of his own time.
His world-famous fairy tales include
The Snow Queen, *The Little Mermaid* and
The Ugly Duckling, and are amongst the most
frequently translated works of literature.
He died in 1875.